D1055498

Chapter books from Henry Holt and Company

*

Boo's Dinosaur
Betsy Byars, illustrated by Erik Brooks

Dragon Tooth Trouble
written and illustrated by Sarah Wilson

Fat Bat and Swoop
written and illustrated by Leo Landry

Little Horse
Betsy Byars, illustrated by David McPhail

Little Horse on His Own
Betsy Byars, illustrated by David McPhail

Maybelle in the Soup
Katie Speck, illustrated by Paul Rátz de Tagyos

Sea Surprise
written and illustrated by Leo Landry

SECOND-GRADE FRIENDS:
The Secret Lunch Special (Book 1)
No More Pumpkins (Book 2)
Peter Catalanotto and Pamela Schembri

Three Little Robbers
Christine Graham, illustrated by Susan Boase

Cinder Rabbit

Lynn E. Hazen

Illustrated by Elyse Pastel

Henry Holt and Company * New York

I am grateful to the talented students and faculty at Vermont College's MFA Program in Writing for Children and Young Adults. Thanks to the MFA's magic—*hippity, bippity, bop*—I, too, can hop! Love and big hugs to fellow writers Lisa Rabe Bose, my E.T., and to every bunny in my great crit groups who patiently watched Cinder flip-flop and hop from rabbit to human to rabbit again and again.

—L. E. H.

Henry Holt and Company, LLC
Publishers since 1866
175 Fifth Avenue
New York, New York 10010
www.HenryHoltKids.com

Library of Congress Cataloging-in-Publication Data
Hazen, Lynn E.
Cinder Rabbit / by Lynn E. Hazen ; illustrated by Elyse Pastel.—1st ed.
p. cm.
Summary: Zoe is chosen for the role of Cinder Rabbit in her school play and is also supposed to lead the class in the Bunny Hop at the end, but ever since wicked Winifred laughed at her for landing in a mud puddle, Zoe has forgotten how to hop.
ISBN-13: 978-0-8050-8194-7 / ISBN-10: 0-8050-8194-1
[1. Self-confidence—Fiction. 2. Theater—Fiction. 3. Rabbits—Fiction.
4. Schools—Fiction.] I. Pastel, Elyse, ill. II. Title.
PZ7.H314977Cin 2008 [E]—dc22 2007027318

First Edition—2008 / Designed by Véronique Lefèvre Sweet
Printed in the United States of America on acid-free paper. ∞
3 5 7 9 10 8 6 4 2

For all my preschool kids and teachers,
especially Rosie and Julian,
for their charm and inspiration

—L. E. H.

For Barry, Josh, and Lily, with love

—E. P.

Contents

* 1 *

Grand Rabbits School

Zoe scurried all the way to Grand Rabbits School.

When the bell rang, every bunny rushed to find a seat.

“Settle down. I know you are excited about our spring play. But, please, stop jumping around,” said Mrs. Lopp.

"Today is Monday. On Friday, we will perform *Cinder Rabbit*," she said. "Let's choose roles."

Zoe took a deep breath as Mrs. Lopp reached into a hat. Zoe's heart beat fast.

Her teacher pulled out a name and announced, "Zoe will be Cinder Rabbit."

"You're going to be the star of the play!" whispered Frida.

Zoe smiled.

"Charlie will be Prince Charming-Whiskers," said Mrs. Lopp.

"Oh man," Charlie said. "I wanted to be the truck driver."

Their teacher assigned the rest of the roles.

“And for the happy ending,” Mrs. Lopp said, “Zoe will lead the Bunny Hop.”

Oh, no, Zoe thought. *I can’t hop.*

* 2 *

Why Can't Zoe Hop?

Zoe worried about hopping while Mrs. Lopp read the play aloud.

Zoe used to hop.

In fact, last week Zoe hopped right into a big mud puddle.

Winifred had laughed at her.

Zoe could still walk and even scurry.

But ever since the mud puddle, Zoe was afraid to hop. She would not even try to hop.

Mrs. Lopp was so busy with all the other bunnies, she had not noticed that Zoe wasn't hopping anymore.

Mrs. Lopp turned to the last page of the play. “And they all lived happily ever after,” she said. “Any questions?”

Charlie waved his paw. "Why can't I be a truck driver?"

"There are no trucks in our spring play," said Mrs. Lopp.

Woody asked, "Who do I get to be?"

Mrs. Lopp checked her list. "You are . . . you are . . . oops!"

"You forgot me," Woody said.

"No," said Mrs. Lopp. "You are—um—the Assistant Director."

Woody smiled and sat up tall.

Zoe was not smiling. Zoe was not sitting up tall. She raised her paw.

"Yes?" said Mrs. Lopp.

"Are you going to teach us how to do the Bunny Hop?" Zoe asked.

Everyone laughed.

"Don't be silly," said her teacher. "Every bunny knows how to hop."

Every bunny but me, Zoe thought.

* 3 *

Worried

Now Zoe worried more than ever.

She asked Frida, “Do *you* want to be Cinder Rabbit? We could trade roles.”

"No," said Frida. "I want to be the fairy god-rabbit. I will get a magic wand."

Zoe asked Winifred, "Do you want to be Cinder Rabbit?"

"No," said Winifred. "I want to be the wicked step-rabbit. I like to be wicked."

Zoe was already worried about hopping. Now she worried about wicked Winifred, too.

the tail of
PLAY

4

Hopscotch

On Tuesday, the class made invitations.

At lunchtime, Zoe was so worried, she couldn't eat her carrot cake.

At recess, she watched Frida play hopscotch. How did she do it? Zoe watched very closely. Frida stood on one foot and bent her knee. Then she hop, hop, hopped.

It looked so easy.

Zoe hid
behind the slide
to practice hopping.
She stood on one
foot. She wobbled.
She wiggled.

Zoe tried to hop, but then she remembered the mud puddle.

Then Winifred swooped down the slide.

"Ya—haa—haaaaa!" Winifred laughed just like a wicked step-rabbit.

I still can't hop, Zoe thought. *I'll try later, when Winifred isn't watching.*

* 5 *

The Dreaded Bunny Hop

On Wednesday, Zoe's class made posters, costumes, and scenery.

Frida made a sparkly magic-carrot wand. Winifred painted a poison apple.

the tail of

"Wrong play," said Frida. She waved her magic wand. "Hippity-bip-pity-bop!" She made the poison apple disappear!

Charlie hid backstage and painted a cardboard truck.

Woody said, "Don't forget me. I'm the Distant Director."

But nobody was listening.

"Line up to practice the Bunny Hop," called Mrs. Lopp. She put Zoe at the front of the line.

Zoe's tummy felt floppity. Her mouth was so dry that she couldn't talk. If she could have talked, she would have said "Stop, because . . . I . . . can't . . . hop!"

6

Hopping Music

Mrs. Lopp plopped down at the piano. She began to play the hopping music.

Plinkety, plinkety.

Plink, plink, plink.

Zoe tried to hop—
but uh-oh!

Plopitty, plopitty.
Plop, plop, PLOP!

All the dancers
fell down in
a heap.

"Oh man," said Charlie. "We should do a play about trucks."

"No," Mrs. Lopp said. "The invitations said *Cinder Rabbit.*"

Frida waved her magic carrot around Zoe. "You can do it, Zoe," said Frida. "Hop!"

Zoe liked Frida. She liked Frida's magic-carrot wand. She liked the magical breeze flowing around her. Maybe it would work. Frida had made the poison apple disappear, hadn't she?

So Zoe took a deep breath and tried again. She tried hopping on her right foot.

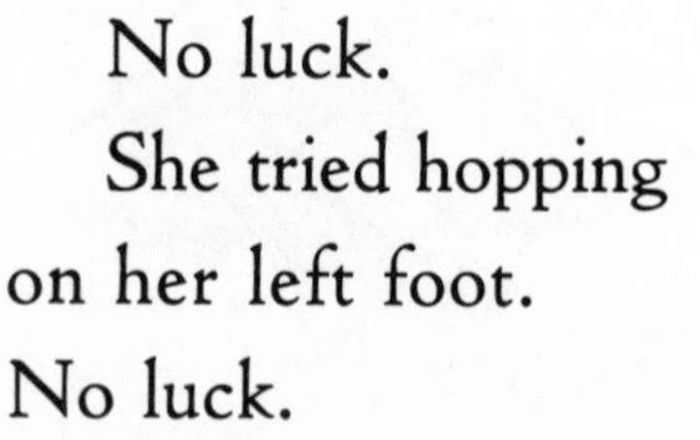

No luck.

She tried hopping on her left foot. No luck.

She even tried jumping with both feet. Still no luck.

Zoe tried again and again.

But when wicked Winifred laughed at her, Zoe stopped trying.

BUNNY BAKERY

7

Downtown

On Thursday, Zoe's class went downtown. They hung posters about the spring play.

Mrs. Lopp lined up the class to return to school.

A shiny blue truck drove up to the crosswalk.

"Oh man," said Charlie. "Look at that big truck!"

Their teacher raised one paw for the truck to stop. Then she waved for her bunnies to go.

"Move it!" said Winifred as she stepped on the back of Zoe's shoe.

Plip!

Zoe's shoe fell off—right in the middle of the crosswalk!

Zoe stood on one foot. The light turned yellow. Her heart beat fast.

The light would soon turn red!

"Hurry, class," said Mrs. Lopp.

Winfred laughed and laughed.

Zoe stood frozen in place as every bunny rushed past her.

Every bunny but Charlie. Charlie grabbed Zoe's shoe and

waved it at the truck driver. When Charlie waved, Zoe's shoe slipped out of his hand and sailed through the air.

Whoosh!

"Oops," said Charlie.

Zoe watched her shoe fly through the sky and bounce off Winifred.

Whoosh-bonk-thonk!

Winifred finally stopped laughing.

The truck driver smiled and waved. *Honk! Hooonk!*

Zoe hopped—all the way to the curb.

"You did it!" said Frida.

"I can hop," said Zoe. "I can hop!"

Her class cheered.

Charlie kneeled to help her. "Here's your shoe, Cinder Rabbit," he said.

Charlie was charming.

Zoe's class was happy. Mrs. Lopp was happy. The truck driver was happy that they were finally out of the crosswalk.

But Zoe was happiest of all. The play could go on!

8

Opening Night

Friday was opening night. The parents were there. The bunnies put on their costumes and scurried into place.

Woody opened the curtain, and the play began.

Zoe remembered all her lines. Winifred was wicked, as usual. Frida was magical.

Charlie was charming.

The play was perfect!

It was time for the Bunny Hop.

The bunnies lined up behind Zoe.

Mrs. Lopp sat at the piano.

Plinkety, plinkety.

Plink, plink, plink.

But, when wicked Winifred laughed, Zoe froze.

"Go," Frida whispered. "Don't listen to Winifred. Just hop!"

"I can't," Zoe gulped. "I forgot how."

Mrs. Lopp began the music again.

Plinkety, plinkety.

Plink, plink.

Plunk!

But Zoe still didn't move.

* 9 *

The Play Must Go On!

"Get the truck!" Woody told Charlie.

"Oh man," Charlie said. "Mrs. Lopp told us NO TRUCKS!"

"*I'm* the Distant Director," said Woody. "I say get the truck!"

Mrs. Lopp peeked around the piano to see what was happening. *Nothing* was happening.

Charlie was missing. Where was Prince Charming-Whiskers?

Mrs. Lopp played the opening music again and again.

Zoe took a deep breath.

Frida waved her magic carrot and said, "Hippity-bippity-bop!"

"I can hop," Zoe told herself. "I did it before and I can do it again!"

She wobbled on one foot and her heart beat faster and faster.

Mrs. Lopp played louder and louder...

Plinkety! Plinkety!

Charlie burst onstage with his cardboard truck.

Plinkety! Plinkety!

"*Honk! Honk! Hooonk!*" shouted Charlie.

"Thanks," said Zoe. She flicked off one shoe, then the other.

Zoe hopped on her right foot.

She hopped on her left foot. Then on both feet. She hopped all the way across the stage with her classmates hopping behind!

10
The End

The audience clapped and cheered.

Zoe smiled her biggest smile.

"Oh man," said Charlie. "That was great!"

"Magical," said Frida.

Even wicked Winifred was impressed.

Zoe was so happy that she hopped right into her parents' arms.

Woody lowered the curtain and said, "And we all lived hoppily ever after."